Tommi: Togger With

By

Stephen J. Ward

Togger Books

For Mr. Sowerby

ISBN 9781446608920

www.toggerbooks.com

A SWEETIE

Someone who cannot kick a togger ball for toffee

A NUTMEG

When a player passes the togger ball between his opponents feet

A VOLLEY

A rather amazing way to score a goal. Striking the ball before it hits the ground

Tommi was walking across the school reception area, when he noticed his Sports Teacher. He was putting up a notice, on the school information board.

"Hello Mr. Sowerby.   Is that the team for Saturday?" said Tommi.

"Yes it is Tommi," replied Mr. Sowerby.

"Am I in it Sir?" he asked.

"Without a doubt," said Mr. Sowerby. "You'll be up front with Sammi Grub – playing as a striker."

"OH NICE!" responded Tommi.

"It's a home game against Appleby Primary," said Mr. Sowerby. "So be here at school at 9.45. Boots polished and raring to go."

"No fear Sir," replied Tommi.

Tommi checked the list to see who else was playing. He noticed that Gruff, Zatt, Munni, Budgie, Clamm and Flimm had also made the team, along with Sniffin, Radjee and Chinn.

"Thanks Sir," Tommi shouted.

Then he was off like a shot, to tell Sammi the good news.

The following Saturday, the Uddersfield Primary togger team gathered in the playground. There they waited for the opposition team to arrive.

"What's the Appleby team like?" asked Sammi.

"They're a bunch of sweeties," responded Gruff. "We thrashed them last year, 4-1."

"Yeah, we could beat them blindfolded," said Zatt cockily. "We'll have no problems at all."

With that the Appleby team bus arrived. The players got off one by one.

"SWEETIES?" questioned Sammi. "They're the

biggest sweeties I've ever seen."

"Crickey!" said Tommi. "Either they've been eating something we haven't, or that's NOT the same team we played before."

"They're... monsters," said Budgie.

"Hey, don't be silly boys. Our opposition must be on the bus still," said Clamm.

"Well if they are, they must be hiding in a very small place," replied Tommi. "The bus looks empty."

All the boys stood on their tiptoes, and strained their necks to get a better look inside the bus.

"OH NO - WE'RE DEAD!" said Budgie. "It's empty - We ARE playing the monsters."

"Not a chance - I'm not - Not in a million years," said Gruff.

"I think I want to go home. I don't feel well," said Zatt.

"Hey before we poop our pants boys, let's get a grip," said Tommi. "I'll ask Mr. Sowerby what's going on."

Tommi walked over to Mr. Sowerby.

"Sir, is that the Appleby team?" he asked.

"It sure is," replied Mr. Sowerby.

"But Sir, aren't they a little bit big?" said Tommi.

"Well the thing is Tommi, there's been a bit of a mistake. Appleby have brought along their year six team," said Mr. Sowerby.

"Yeah, that's a bit of a mistake alright," said Tommi. "Seeing as we're only the year three team."

"It'll be alright," said Mr. Sowerby.

"It will?" said Tommi. "So...the games off then?"

"No, of course not," replied Mr. Sowerby.

"But..." said Tommi.

"They're here now.   So we might as well make a game of it," said Mr. Sowerby.

"But..." said Tommi.

"It'll be a great experience for our lads," said Mr. Sowerby, enthusiastically.

"BUT!..." said Tommi.

"YES, character building stuff, that's what it'll be," continued Mr. Sowerby.

14

"But...," said Tommi.

"Alright Tommi, let's get cracking. Get the team into the changing room," said Mr. Sowerby, as he walked away.

Tommi walked back to his friends in a daze.

"Well, what's the word Tommi?" asked Gruff.

"That word would be - DOOMED. Think Sowerby has lost the plot there somewhere," replied Tommi.

"WHAT! So we're playing them then?" asked Clamm.

Tommi nodded.

"Mummy," whimpered Budgie.

Tommi reluctantly lead the team to the changing room. There they changed, very, very quietly. The next thing they knew they were out on the pitch, facing Appleby.

"COME ON UDDERSFIELD," rallied Tommi.

"We look like a bunch of sweeties," said Gruff, "We're going to get thrashed."

"Yeah, it looks like they could beat us blindfolded," said Zatt.

"Yes they do," said Tommi. "But it doesn't mean we should roll over and play dead."

Gruff and Zatt grumbled and chuntered.

"Look, alright, they're big, and mean looking, and ugly," said Tommi. "But as far as we know, Sammi's sisters could be better players than that lot."

"I'll swap places with one of Sammi's sisters then," said Zatt.

Tommi frowned.

"Look what I'm saying is if we are going to lose, let's show a little backbone. Let's just do the

best WE can, ok," said Tommi.

"Yeah, that's right Tommi," said Gruff. "And at Monday's assembly, when the Headmaster reads out the score to the whole school – My battered and bruised body will feel SO proud, that we only lost 25-nil, rather than, 26-NIL."

Tommi felt that he was fighting a losing battle with his own team. So he jogged over to the only player he trusted.

"Sammi, I'm worried. It looks like the team is defeated before we even start the game," he said.

"I think so Tommi. Never mind, how about

me and you doing what we're best at ?" replied Sammi.

Tommi smiled.

"Good answer Sammi," said Tommi. "GOOD answer."

Mr. Sowerby was refereeing the game. He blew his whistle to start it off.

Unfortunately for Uddersfield, Appleby were much better than Sammi's sisters.
They also made some of the third year boys, look like proper sweeties.

Within no time Appleby had put the ball past

Budgie in goal, to score.

"HA, HA, HA, HA," laughed the Appleby centre forward. "This is SO easy. They're rubbish."

Gruff looked angry.

"Don't like being laughed at, Zatt," said Gruff.

"Don't like being called rubbish, Gruff," said Zatt.

"Don't like being a sweetie, either," said Budgie.

"Time we started playing real togger then lads," said Tommi.

26

"Yes – it – is," said Gruff, a lot more determined.

Mr. Sowerby started the game off again. The ball was played back to Gruff in midfield.

Gruff passed the ball to Sammi, on the left wing.

Sammi then did what Sammi did best, dribbling the ball around three of the Appleby players.

Once he'd made it to the goal-line, he chipped the ball across to Zatt at the far post.

Zatt had two defenders marking him. But he out leapt them both, heading the ball into the path of Tommi.

28

Tommi ran in fast and volleyed it into the back of the goal.

"WEEEEEEEEEE-HEEEEEEEEE!" squealed Zatt, running around with his arms out like a fly gone mad.

Gruff approached the Appleby centre forward. "Whose rubbish now laughing boy," he said.

For the rest of the game, Uddersfield played with the same kind of determination.

Tommi got another two goals. But in the end, Appleby ended up the winners by four goals to three.

"Well done Uddersfield," said Mr. Sowerby. "Very well done lads, I couldn't be more proud of you all. You really showed great character against a team with much stronger players. I can't wait to tell the Headmaster about this."

The Appleby team showed their respect also. They lined up and applauded and cheered the Uddersfield lads back into the changing room.

"Sorry Tommi," said Gruff. "You were right. If we'd listened to you in the first place, we might have drawn that game, 3-3."

"Yes, that maybe so Gruff," said Tommi. "But the good thing is, at least we've proven something

more important."

"What's that mate?" asked Gruff.

"That none of us play togger like sweeties," replied Tommi.

Both Tommi and Gruff laughed. Then they joined the rest of the team, to celebrate the game that they had just lost.

FINAL WHISTLE

Printed in Great Britain
by Amazon